South African animals

by Lindiwe Mabuza

illustrated by Alan Baker

Tamarind

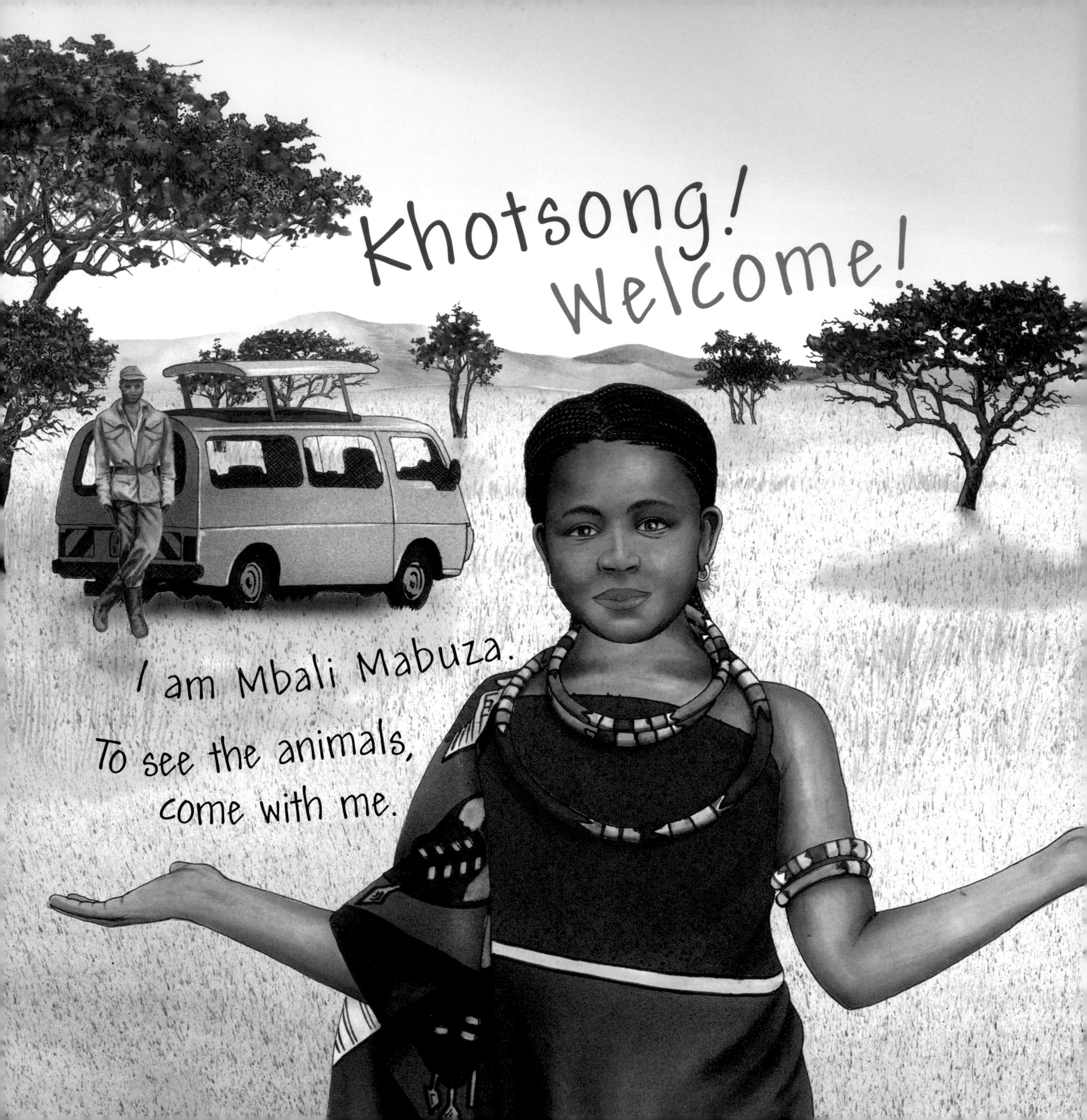

Khotsong!
Welcome!

I am Mbali Mabuza.

To see the animals,
come with me.

In our beautiful land these animals roam,
Here in South Africa, this is my home.

Aardvark feeds in the dead of night.

Buffaloes roam in the warm sunlight.

Hungry **cheetah**

hopes for a meal.

Dolphins dance and twirl and wheel.

Bath time for **elephants** is wonderful fun.

Flycatcher darts in the noonday sun.

Giraffes look down
heads high above ground.

Hippopotamus feeds on sweet grass he has found.

Ibis and impalas are graceful and quick.

Jackal frightens mother bird's chick.

There's plenty of grass
for curly-horned **Kudu**.

Leopard has eaten, now he watches **lion** chew.

Many-legged **millipede**

marches by day.

Night jar
screeches,

night adder
is at play.

Ostriches have wings they cannot use.

Penguins can walk

or swim as they choose.

The extinct **quagga** is no longer with us.

But we are happy to have **rhinoceros**.

These **seals** are playing

or is it a fight?

Tree dassie's screams wake up the night.

Umsumpe

is the Zulu name for this deer.

Viper is invisible until I am near.

Whales sing aloud in the ocean clear.

Xhama is the Xhosa name for this deer.

and last come the **zebras**...
what a wonderful sight!

South African animals

South Africa is a vast country at the tip of Africa. The most well-known animals that live here are the "Big Five": elephant, rhino, leopard, lion and buffalo. South Africa is also home to many different people and there are 11 official languages. The animals have names in each of the different languages.

Aardvark (the name means "earth pig" in Afrikaans) – a small, strong mammal that hunts at night. It uses its powerful claws to tear open termite mounds. It traps the insects on its long, sticky tongue or sucks them into its mouth.

Buffalo – one of the most dangerous of South Africa's "Big Five". A buffalo will attack without giving any warning. Buffaloes live in huge herds of up to 2,000 cows, bulls and calves, and are very peaceful among themselves.

Cheetah – the fastest land animal in the world, it can reach almost 100km per hour. Its claws do not retract (pull in) all the way, giving it extra grip when it runs. Unlike other big cats, a cheetah does not roar.

Dolphin (Bottlenose) – a strong, stocky mammal that lives all its life in the water. Dolphins live in big groups, called schools. They play together as they swim, often nudging each other and rubbing snouts.

Elephant (African) – the largest living land animal. Its muscly trunk works as a nose, a hand and even an extra foot. It uses its trunk to communicate, gather food, and spurt water and dust. It can delicately stroke a baby or pull a tree right out of the ground! An African elephant has large ears.

Flycatcher – a songbird often seen in woodland and gardens. It is a noisy bird with a harsh call. It eats insects, hunting as it flies.

Giraffe – an amazing-looking animal, with a long neck and legs. It has to spread its front legs to reach the ground to drink. But it can also pluck leaves from the tallest trees. Its height helps it to keep an eye on its family and spot danger from a long way away.

Hippopotamus – a huge mammal that spends most of its time in water, with just its eyes, ears and nostrils peeping out. It must keep out of the sun so as not to get its thin skin sunburned. It feeds on grass at night.

Ibis (Hadeda) – a large bird with a long, curved beak. It pokes around in the mud for small fish, shrimp and shellfish. It screeches "har, har, har" as it flies, which is what gave it its name.

Impala – a graceful, slender antelope that lives in all kinds of environments. It eats young grass shoots in the wet season, and herbs and shrubs at other times. The females live together in herds in an area of land claimed by a dominant male.

Jackal – a meat-eater that looks a little like a dog or a fox. It eats anything, from young antelopes to sheep, reptiles, insects and birds that nest on the ground, such as guinea fowl (in the picture). If it cannot find any meat, it will even eat fruit, berries and grass.

Kudu – a big, beautiful antelope. The males have long, twisted horns that grow to more than 1.5m. Walking through trees, they lift their chin so their horns lay flat against their back and do not get caught in the branches.

Leopard – a big cat with a spotted coat that hunts alone at dawn or dusk. It eats anything, from insects to giraffe or buffalo calves. It can climb trees to look for prey, to hunt, or have a rest. It stores its prey high up on a branch to keep it safe from other animals.

Lion – the king of the big cats! An adult lion's roar can be heard a long way away. Lions laze around most of the day. In the cool of the early morning, the lionesses hunt together. The lion gets the best share of the food, even though he does not usually join in the hunt.

Millipede (African giant black) – a beautiful, gentle insect that curls up into a ball when it is scared. This millipede is one of the largest in the world and can grow as thick as a man's thumb. It is not harmful, though it can give off a liquid that stings.

Nightjar (Fiery necked) – a small bird that hunts moths and other large, flying insects at night. It does not make a nest, but just lays its eggs on the ground. Its brown and white feathers camouflage it well.

Night adder (Common) – a poisonous snake that hunts frogs at night. It will hiss and strike out if annoyed or threatened. Its bite is poisonous but will not kill a human.

Ostrich – the tallest bird in the world! It has tiny wings (but can't fly!) and a very long neck and legs. It has two toes, the bigger one like a hoof. This helps it to run fast and kick hard. The males, which are black and white, help the females look after their babies.

Penguin (African or Jackass) – a small bird that cannot fly but uses its wings to swim through the water. It has shiny, waterproof feathers that help to keep its skin dry.

Quagga – a kind of zebra that lived in the desert and was hunted to extinction in the 1870s. Scientists in South Africa have started a breeding programme to try and bring the quagga back, so we may be seeing them again soon.

Rhinoceros (Black) – a huge, horned mammal that eats grass and shrubs. It has bad eyesight but a good sense of hearing and of smell. It looks heavy and clumsy, but can run at speeds of up to 60km per hour.

Seal (Cape fur) – a large sea mammal that lives on rocky shorelines. A Cape fur seal can swim up to 160km out to sea to hunt the fish it eats. On land, it uses its flippers to waddle along.

Tree dassie – a small but thickset, plant-eating mammal. It is a great climber and in the day it shelters in the hollow of a tree. It comes out at night to find food, barking, growling and squeaking noisily.

Umsumpe (in Zulu; the English name is **Red duiker**, which uses an Afrikaans word meaning "diver") – a tiny, shy antelope (45cm high) that lives in woods. When it is frightened it dives into the bushes to hide, which is how it got its name.

Viper (**Gaboon**) – a rainforest snake that lives camouflaged in the leaves of the forest floor. It spends most of its time totally still, waiting for prey to pass by. It can strike with great speed and agility.

Whale (Southern right) – a huge sea mammal that visits the coast of South Africa in spring to have its babies. In the southern hemisphere the seasons happen at the opposite time of the year to the northern hemisphere, so spring is in October. The whales live in the Antarctic Ocean the rest of the year.

Xhama (the English name is **Red hartebeest** which uses an Afrikaans word meaning "strong animal") – a tall, elegant antelope that lives in herds of 20 to 300 animals. The herd is usually made up of a bull, some females and their calves, as well as some young bulls. The bulls fight during the mating season.

Yellow-billed hornbill – a medium-sized bird with a large, curved, yellow beak that looks a little like a cow's horn. It eats small seeds, insects and spiders that it picks up from the ground.

Yellow-billed kite – a large, hunting bird (bird of prey) that is an excellent flier. It spends hours riding the wind, only occasionally flapping its wings. It can swoop and dive impressively.

Zebra – a horse-like animal with a striped coat. Each zebra has a different pattern of stripes. Its black mane is made of short hairs that stand up straight and its tail has a tuft at the tip.

Dedicated to all the children of Africa
L.W.

To my sister Suzie, with love
A.B.

Thanks to Mbali Mabuza

Published by Tamarind Ltd, 2007
PO Box 52
Northwood
Middx HA6 1UN

www.tamarindbooks.co.uk

Text © Lindiwe Mabuza
Illustrations © Alan Baker
Edited by Simona Sideri

ISBN: 978-1-870516-85-3

Printed in Singapore